Lost in the
Blizzard

written by Constance Horne
illustrated by Lori McGregor McCrae

A Hodgepog Book

Hodgepog Books and The Books Collective acknowledge the ongoing support of the Canada Council for the Arts and the Alberta Foundation for the Arts for our publishing program. We also acknowledge the support of the City of Edmonton and the Edmonton Arts Council

Editors for Press:
Mary Woodbury, Glen Huser, Luanne Armstrong

Cover design by Robert Woodbury
Inside layout by Dianne J. Cooper at The Books Collective
in Times New Roman, Arial Black and Palatino (True-Type Font)
in Windows Quark X-Press 4.0.
Printed at Hignell Press

A Hodgepog Book for Kids

Published in Canada by Hodgepog Books, a member of:
The Books Collective,
214-21 10405 Jasper Avenue,
Edmonton, Alberta, T5J 3S2.
Telephone (780) 448 0590

Canadian Cataloguing in Publishing Data
Horne, Constance
Lost in the Blizzard

ISBN 1895836-69-7

I. McCrae, Lori McGregor, 1958- II. Title
PS8565.O6693L67 1999   jC813'.54   C99-910697-X
PZ7.H7824Lo 1999

5637

LOST IN THE BLIZZARD
by Constance Horne

TABLE OF CONTENTS

Chapter One

STORM WARNING

On March 4th, 1966, Miss Maxwell's grade five class were so busy with their science lesson on weather that none of them noticed that a real storm was building up outside. They were all surprised when the principal's voice came over the loudspeaker. It was only eleven o'clock in the morning, but she told them that school was dismissed for the day.

"A very bad storm is headed toward the city," she said.

Marnie Carder looked out the window. A squall of snow rattled the glass. She jumped and the children around her laughed.

"Fraidy-cat!" whispered Paul from behind her.

That wasn't fair. Marnie had just moved to Winnipeg from Victoria one week ago. She could only remember two years when it snowed in the winter and that had been gentle, wet flakes, not like the hard pellets that had just hit the window.

"Pay attention," said Miss Maxwell sternly.

The principal went on. "All children are to leave school immediately. You will have time to get home before the worst of the storm hits. But don't loiter! If you can't go home, go to a neighbour's or a friend's house. Let your teacher know where you are going and what the telephone number is. Teachers, be sure to get this information from each child. Children, you older ones take your younger brothers and sisters with you. Go straight home. I repeat, the storm is going to be very severe. Go quickly."

Miss Maxwell checked to make sure that snow boots were zipped up, parka strings tied and mitten cuffs tucked into sleeves. As they filed past, she spoke to each boy and girl. When it was her turn, Marnie showed the house key on a string around her neck.

"My mother works," she said shyly, "but she always comes home and has lunch with my little brother and me."

2

Miss Maxwell tilted her head to look through the bottom part of her glasses. She fastened the stiff snap of Marnie's red parka.

"Have you ever been in a snow storm, Marnie?" she asked.

"No, Miss Maxwell. We didn't have much snow on Vancouver Island."

"Well, you're going to remember your first week in Winnipeg," said the teacher. She tied Marnie's red and white scarf then rested her thin hands on the girl's shoulders.

Marnie looked up. The thought of playing in the snow was one of the things that had helped her most when she was sad about leaving their home in Victoria. But the strangeness of being sent home early and the look on the teacher's face frightened her. She said nothing.

"A good snowstorm can be fun, Marnie, but a blizzard is a serious thing. It can be dangerous. Promise me you'll go straight home."

"I promise, Miss Maxwell."

"Good!" The teacher patted Marnie's shoulder twice. "Run along now and find your little brother," she said.

Chris was dancing back and forth in the doorway of the grade two room. As soon as he saw Marnie, he raced off down the hall to the outside door. Marnie stopped to promise once again that she would take him straight home.

Outside, it was snowing fast. From the top of the school steps Marnie looked down the street. She couldn't see Chris through the snow. A sudden gust of wind took her breath away. She turned with her back to the wind and saw Chris racing off in the wrong direction.

"Come back, Chris!" she screamed.

He shouted something, but kept going.

Why can't he ever do as he's told, thought Marnie. He heard what the principal said.

4

She stared after him. The wind slapped her scarf against her face. She shivered. She wanted to be safe and warm at home with her mother.

As she watched, Chris caught up to a little boy in a green parka and turned the corner with him. Marnie hurried after them. The hard-packed crust under the new snow was slippery. Pushed by the wind, she skated rather than ran. It would have been fun, if she hadn't been so mad at Chris. Halfway down the block she overtook him as he plodded along beside his friend.

"Where do you think you're going?" she asked.

"To Bobby's," he answered. "He's got a hundred toy cars."

"Nearly a hundred," muttered Bobby into his scarf.

"You can't go!" said Marnie. "The principal said we have to go home."

"I will, after I've seen his cars," Chris answered.

By this time, they had reached the next street. By turning right at this corner, they would be heading toward their own house. Marnie stopped. Snow was still falling and it was much colder.

"Come on, Chris," she said. "You've got lots of cars at home."

If he answered, the wind blew his words away. When he was younger, Chris could sometimes be made to follow if Marnie pretended to walk away from him. She tried the trick now.

"Goodbye, Chris," she yelled into the wind. "I'm going home."

She took a few steps along the street, being careful not to look back. When she did turn around, icy pellets stung her face and she had to close her eyes. She pulled her scarf over her mouth, put her mittened hand over her eyes and peered around. She could see nothing but snow.

Frightened, she struggled back to the corner and found the two boys leaning against a telephone pole to rest.

Some teenagers came out of the storm.

"Is that you, Bobby?" asked one of them. "Come on, you can walk with us."

"I guess you better go home," said Bobby to Chris.

"Okay," answered Chris.

"At last!" cried Marnie.

✽ ✽ ✽

Chapter Two

LOST IN THE STORM

Marnie grabbed Chris' arm and dragged him in the direction of home. He stumbled along beside her for a few steps before pulling her to a stop. She turned and glared at him.

"I'm tired, Marnie," he said. "It's hard to walk in the snow."

7

Marnie thought of several things to say to him, but there was no use talking in that wind. Besides, he really looked very tired and cold. Last Sunday had been a clear, crisp day and their mother had taken them for a walk to show them the neighbourhood. Both of the children had been surprised at the flat prairie landscape. They could see miles and miles of snow-covered fields at the edge of the city. Marnie remembered that there were vacant lots on this street. She decided to take a shortcut across one of them.

She wished she could see clearly. It would be awful to walk into a stranger's yard and get yelled at.

She brushed some icicles off Chris' scarf and pulled it up over his nose. Taking him more gently by the hand, she led him forward until she was sure they had passed all the houses. Then she turned into a vacant lot and directly into the wind. It had been hard to walk on the sidewalk. Here, in the softer snowdrifts of the open field, it was even harder. She had to drop Chris' hand. With every step, snow came over their boot tops. Marnie soon knew she had made a mistake by taking the shortcut.

"Why did we come this way?" Chris mumbled. "Let's go back to the sidewalk."

"No!" shouted Marnie over the wind. "Keep going! We'll soon be out to the other street."

Just then, Chris stumbled into a hole up to his waist. In trying to get out, he fell face down. Marnie made a grab for his leg and fell on top of him, pushing

8

him farther into the snow. After a struggle, she stood up and turned her brother onto his back. She helped him clear snow from his eyes and nose.

"Why did you do that?" he asked crossly.

"I didn't do it on purpose! Get up!"

She pulled him to his feet and brushed him off. He screwed up his face and sniffed.

"Don't cry!" said Marnie. "Your face will freeze."

She looked around. Nothing to see but snow and

nothing to hear but the wind. Miss Maxwell's words came back to her. 'A snow storm is dangerous.' They must hurry home. Which way was home? Remembering that the wind had been blowing in their faces, Marnie told Chris to hold the hem of her parka and walk behind her. That way, her body sheltered him a little from the wind. Then she turned into it, tucked in her chin and plowed ahead. In a few minutes the wind changed right around and began to push them forward. Marnie knew then that she could not trust the wind to tell her which way to go. But she could see no landmarks. Which way was home?

They plodded on. After what seemed a very long time, Marnie again felt hard snow under her feet. They were out of the vacant lot on a bit of the road that the wind had cleared. She stamped hard to knock the snow from her boots. There was no feeling in her feet. They seemed to have turned to two rocks at the end of her legs. Chris just stood quietly beside her.

"Are you okay?" she asked him.

He nodded.

"It can't be much farther now. Can you make it?"

"Yes," he mumbled through his scarf. "Let's go."

"Good boy!" she said.

That's what Mummy always called him. Oh, if only they were home with Mummy now!

They came to a crossroad. Marnie was sure it couldn't be their street. They hadn't walked far enough. She kept on straight ahead. As long as the road was clear, she held Chris' hand and walked beside him. Soon, they hit drifts again and Chris walked behind in her footsteps. The drifts puzzled Marnie because the roads around their house had been plowed before the storm. Why was there so much snow?

The wind dropped for a few seconds and she paused to catch her breath. She tried to peer through the snow. Surely they were near home now! At first she could see nothing. Then Chris pointed to a light on top of a black iron post.

"Look, Marnie! We saw that lantern on Sunday!"

"Then it's not far now," said Marnie. "Come on!"

Marnie did not want to upset Chris but she knew that there were many lanterns like that in the neighbourhood.

The little boy struggled on almost happily for a few more minutes. Then he whimpered. Marnie wanted to shout at him to shut up but she knew that would only make him cry harder. She felt like crying herself. They must be going the wrong way. It shouldn't take this long to get home. They stumbled into a fence post. Chris leaned against it.

He said, "Let's go into this house."

"No!" his sister answered crossly. "We don't know the people who live here."

"I'm cold, Marnie!"

"I know. So am I."

For a moment she thought longingly of a warm

room out of the wind. But she was too shy to ask strangers for help.

"It can't be far now," she coaxed.

"That's what you said before!"

As soon as they stepped away from the white fence, it was swallowed up in the storm. There seemed to be nothing in the world but the two of them, endlessly plodding along against the wind. An extra hard gust blew Chris down. He sat with bowed head while snow swirled around him. Marnie stared at him. She wanted to plop down beside him. Her legs were trembling with tiredness and her forehead ached with the cold.

"Get up," she said.

"I'm too tired," he answered.

She watched helplessly as a tiny drift built up on one of his boots. She knew he shouldn't sit there, but she was too tired to pull him up.

"Please get up, Chris," she begged. "We'll go into the next house we come to."

"Promise?"

"Yes," she said, thinking that no stranger could be more frightening than this storm.

Chris pushed himself up and they went on. In a few minutes, he bumped into the corner of a building.

"Marnie! Marnie! It's a house!" he yelled.

❧　❧　❧

Chapter Three

SHELTER

Marnie reached above her brother's head and felt a wall. He was right! A house! Shelter! Warmth! They could phone Mummy to come and take them home.

"Find the door," she said.

She put both hands on the wall and slipped along sideways 'til she came to some steps. They were drifted over. Almost too tired to climb herself, she had to pull Chris up with her. She knocked on the door. No one answered.

The wind is so noisy, she thought. Maybe they couldn't hear the knock. She banged hard with both mittens. Still no answer. Chris turned around and kicked the door with his heels.

"Don't!" said Marnie. "That's rude."

"I don't care," said Chris and kicked again. For a moment Marnie hoped that no one was home.

Chris slid down and sat with his back to the door.

"You promised we'd go in," he said in a tired voice.

Marnie looked at him. He couldn't go any further. She turned the doorknob. The wind blew the door wide open, slamming it against the inside wall. Chris tumbled in and Marnie followed. Together they struggled to close the door against the wind.

If anyone was home they must have heard that. Marnie turned around, half expecting to face an angry grown-up.

13

The house was empty: no furniture, no carpets, no curtains. The walls were grey plaster and the floors were bare plywood.

"Nobody lives here," she told Chris. "It's a new house — not even finished yet."

Her voice echoed in the empty room. She took a few steps forward. They stood in what would be the L-shaped living-dining room. Along the same wall as the door was a large picture window, now covered half way up by a snowdrift. There was a red brick fireplace in the end wall. On the back wall, opposite the front window, was a small window set high up. Through it Marnie could see snow whirling past.

I don't remember any new houses near our town-house, she thought. We're lost!

Chris pulled her sleeve.

"I don't like it here," he said. "It's cold and there's no people. I want to go home!" A fat bubble of fear burst somewhere in Marnie's insides. She turned on him in a fury.

"It's your fault!" she shouted. "If it wasn't for you, we would be home. You're a nut! Not even a peanut. A great, big, fat Brazil nut!"

He began to cry.

At once, she was sorry. She pulled him to her and hugged him.

"Don't cry! Don't cry! I'll take care of you."

❈   ❈   ❈

MRS. CARDER

Soon after the first storm warning was broadcast on the radio, stores and offices all over the city emptied as people tried to outrace the blizzard. Marnie and Chris' mother was a hairdresser in a beauty salon in the shopping plaza not far from where they lived. As soon as she heard the schools were closing, she hurried home. Her children were not there.

⁂

At 12:30 p.m., she phoned the police. They got in touch with Miss Maxwell who phoned the Grade Five pupils. Greta Williams remembered that she had seen Marnie running after her little brother, who was walking with Bobby Maddox. Bobby told about saying goodbye on the street corner. No one had seen the children since then.

⁂

At 2:30 p.m., the first bulletin about the children was read on the radio. "Marnie and Chris Carder are missing. Police think they may have become lost in the storm and taken shelter somewhere. If you live near Prairie View School, would you please check your garage, shed, porch or even your car, if it isn't buried yet."

⁂

Chapter Four

WARMTH

When Marnie hugged Chris, their icy scarves stuck together. She had to pull hard to get away from him. The wet wool made her face itchy. She took off her scarf and mittens and helped Chris remove his. She put them on the half-wall that separated the entrance hall from the living room. The mittens stood up

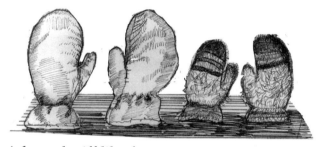

straight and stiff like four snow covered soldiers.

In one corner of the room a broom leaned above a small pile of building rubble. Marnie used it to sweep the snow off Chris and handed him the broom to do the same for her. Because they were out of the wind, it felt warmer. But the house was cold. The snow did not melt on the floor. When they spoke, they could see their breath.

They could freeze to death, even in the house.

"Let's move around," said Marnie. "Stamp your feet." She led him in a march around the empty living

17

room. "Swing your arms! Are you any warmer?"

"A little," answered Chris.

Marnie blew on her hands and rubbed them together.

"If there was a phone, where would it be?"she asked.

"In the hall," said Chris.

He ran up and down looking for it, although Marnie could see no telephone.

"In the kitchen!" he shouted.

They found a hole in the wall with wires sticking out, but no phone. Beside this hole was a wall switch. Marnie clicked it and the light came on.

"Oh, boy!" Chris shouted.

He clicked another switch by an open door and turned on the light on the basement landing. He stepped down three steps and looked into the basement. Marnie joined him. When the house was finished, the back door would open on to this landing. Right now, there was no door. Pieces of plywood had been laid over the opening and heavy boards nailed across to keep them in place.

Chris said, "There's a furnace. Should we go down and see if it works?"

Marnie looked into the dark basement. She couldn't go down into that blackness. Something horrible might be down there.

"Let's see the rest of the house first," she said.

A bathroom and three bedrooms opened off a long hallway. The doors had not been hung. They leaned against the wall on one side of the passage. There was

18

a light in the bathroom but none in the bedrooms. The windows were set so high above their heads that all they could see was blowing snow.

While they were exploring the house, the wind howled and raged. In the back bedroom a new sound was added to the din. It was a low moaning that built up to a scream and then faded. Before it quite ended, it would begin to build again. Chris stared at Marnie with frightened eyes. She gulped and pulled him out of the room.

"What is it?" he asked in a whisper.

"The wind," answered Marnie. But what was it really?

Chris was looking over his shoulder as he walked down the hall. He bumped into a door. It fell with a thud. Marnie jumped.

"You nut!" she screamed. "Watch where you're going!"

"I didn't mean to," said Chris.

"Help me put it back," said Marnie.

The door was not as heavy as it looked, but their cold hands made it hard to lift. When it was upright once more, Chris was whimpering.

" I don't like this place," he said.

" Neither do I," said Marnie.

She took his hand and led him back to the living room.

" We have to stay here until the storm is over, Chris. You don't want to go out there again, do you?"

"I want to go home," he said with a sob.

"We can't go home. I don't know where home is. We're lost!"

The little boy cried harder and Marnie looked at him sadly. She, too, was cold and hungry and frightened. She would like to cry, too. She wished she could feel Mummy's arms around her and hear her voice saying that she'd take care of them. But when Mummy wasn't there, she expected Marnie to take care of Chris. If only they could get warm!

"Show me the furnace you saw, Chris. Maybe it works."

Chris rubbed his hand across his eyes and led the way down the steps to the basement landing. Side by side, they walked down three more steps. One small electric bulb at the foot of the stairs made a pool of light in the dark cellar. The howling of the wind was not so strong here but the same moaning sound that they heard in the bedroom came from the far corner.

"See, there's the furnace," said Chris.

"Yes," answered Marnie slowly. "I see it, but it doesn't look finished. See those pipes against the wall?"

Chris went down another step and leaned over the railing.

"Yeah, you're right. It isn't put together. Too bad. There's some wood we could have burned. See?"

Marnie could make out a pile of building rubbish

in the dimness.

"There's a fireplace upstairs," she said. "Maybe we could start a fire there."

"Yeah!" said Chris brightly. "Let's go see!"

Back in the living room, Marnie stared down at cold, grey ashes and a partly burned piece of thin wood.

"Somebody had a fire here," she said.

She remembered holidays at her grandparents' summer cottage at Gimli. There was a wood-burning stove in the kitchen and a fireplace in the living room. Every morning, Marnie helped Grandpa to fill the two wood boxes. On cold evenings she helped to lay the wood in the fireplace. She always had to stand back.

"Grandpa could build a fire here," said Chris.

"No one can make a fire without matches," Marnie answered.

She looked up and saw the bright blue cover of a book of matches on the mantelpiece. She snatched it down and opened it. There were eight matches left.

"Help me bring the junk from the corner," she said.

There were torn scraps of building paper, broken wooden laths, some with plaster still clinging to them, and small chunks of 2 x 4's. The children made a small mound in the fireplace. Marnie tore a match out of the book. It bent out of shape and wouldn't light. The second lit with such a flash that Marnie dropped it in fright. It went out.

"Let me try!" said Chris.

"No, there aren't many left. We can't waste any."

"You wasted two!"

Marnie didn't want him to cry again, so she said, "Okay, you can try this one. Only one, then it's my

turn again."

Chris crouched down, quickly struck the match, cupped the flame with his hand and carefully held it to a bit of the paper until it caught fire. In a few minutes, the pile was blazing.

" Super!" said Marnie.

Then the flame died down and smoke poured into the room. Chris coughed and moved back.

"It's going to go out!" wailed Marnie.

She remembered that Grandpa had told her a fire needed air to burn. He had showed her the draft hole in the chimney in the cottage fireplace. She felt around in this fireplace, found a metal handle and pushed hard. At once, the wind rushed down the chimney and nearly blew out the flame. Marnie closed the draft part way and the fire burned steadily.

Both of them watched it carefully for a few minutes. Then Chris laughed.

"I told you I could light it," he said.

For the first time since leaving school, Marnie smiled. The fire would warm them, they could have a rest and, when the storm was over, they could go out and ask someone to phone their mother. That thought made Marnie sad again. Mummy would be worried about them. She might scold when they got home.

But it was Chris' fault, not hers.

❄   ❄   ❄

Chapter Five

Chris' Good Idea

Soon Marnie had another worry. The paper and thin wood burned much too quickly.

"We need some bigger wood," she said.

"There was lots in the basement," said Chris.

They went back to the landing and peered into the cellar. No light at all came through the snow-covered windows. The bulb at the foot of the stairs only made the corners seem darker and spookier.

Chris looked at his big sister. "It's pretty dark down there."

Marnie took a deep breath. "It sure is. But we have to keep the fire burning. Let's go."

At the rubbish pile, Marnie made Chris fill her arms with pieces of 2 x 4's. Then she told him to gather up chunks of pink insulation and smaller scraps of wood.

They hurried back upstairs and rebuilt the fire. The insulation scraps burned very slowly and gave lots of heat.

"Bring our scarves and mittens, Chris," Marnie said. "They'll dry out by the fire and be ready when we need them."

Chris laid the four stiff mittens in a row on the hearth while Marnie hung the scarfs from the mantelpiece. She used a block of wood to hold them in place.

24

Chris crouched over the fire warming his hands.

"Listen, Marnie," he said. "The mittens are sizzling like sausages. I wish they were sausages. I'm hungry."

"There's no use being hungry," she answered crossly. "We haven't got anything to eat."

Chris was quiet for a moment and then he asked, "When can we go home?"

"I don't know," answered Marnie. "Listen to the wind! Look at the snow out there! We'll have to wait 'til the storm's over."

"I want Mummy," said Chris with a whimper.

25

Marnie was also hungry and frightened and that made her angry. "Don't be such a baby!" she said.

"I'm not a baby. I just want to go home where it's warm."

"It's warm here," answered Marnie.

"No, it's not!" said Chris. "My front's getting warm, but my back is freezing."

His sister frowned. It was true. The little fire was not doing much to warm the icy air.

"It's because the room is so big and there's no door to shut," she said. "But we can't make the fire too big or we'll run out of stuff to burn."

"I wish we could make a fort with blankets and chairs like we do at home. Only there's no blankets and chairs." He thought for a moment. "Hey, Marnie! I know!" he yelled.

"What?"

"Those doors! We could make a fort with them."

He ran noisily down the hall. Marnie followed.

"How?" she asked.

"Just prop 'em around the fireplace."

"But they're too heavy!"

"No, they're not," said Chris. "We'll drag them along. Help me."

The sound of wood scraping on wood drowned out the shrieking of the wind for the next few minutes.

At each end of the fireplace the children leaned a door upright against the mantelpiece. But they could not make another door lean on that one without pushing the first one over. So, they

26

placed the next two on their sides. They now had a shelter less than a meter high on the long side. They could get in and out by sliding one door along the floor.

They carried all the fuel inside their little shelter and Marnie piled it into two neat piles, one on either side of the hearth. She turned the mittens over to toast on the other side and turned the scarfs end for end. Chris put more wood on the fire and they settled down with their backs to the new wall.

"It's lots warmer," said Chris.

"Yes, it is," agreed Marnie. "That was a good idea you had."

Chris grinned, then stared quietly at the flames for a few minutes.

"What are we going to do now, Marnie?" he asked.

She groaned. What were they going to do? It would be a long afternoon if the storm kept up 'til supper time. She had no idea what time it was except that it was long past lunch time.

Chapter Six

TERROR IN THE DARK

Marnie was used to taking care of Chris. She had been doing it most of his life. She knew he was happiest when he was busy. But, what was there to do here? She watched him put another block of wood on the fire.

"First we'd better fetch more wood from the basement," she said.

As soon as they stepped away from their cozy nook, they knew how lucky they were to have a fire. Their breath hung in the cold air.

Even though they carried back as big a load as they could, the piles looked very small to Marnie.

"We'll have to go for more," she said.

When they were halfway down the steps for the third time, a fierce gust of wind struck so hard that the whole house seemed to shudder. Chris started back up, but Marnie grabbed his hand and led him quickly down the steps and over to the corner.

"Hurry," she said. "Take a great big load so we don't have to come back."

Suddenly, Chris paused with his arms half full of insulation scraps. A long, low moan came from the far corner.

"What's that?" he whispered.

Marnie, too, stood still, staring round-eyed in the direction of the sound.

"It's the wind. Just the same as we heard before," she answered quietly. "Only louder. Hurry up!"

The children were several metres apart. Marnie was squatting down, balancing pieces of wood on one arm while she picked up new pieces with the other hand. Chris was trying to get his arms around a big pile of scraps he had gathered. Suddenly, the moan was cut off by a great thud.

The lights went out!

"Marnie! Marnie! Marnie!" screamed Chris.

Terror kept Marnie frozen for a moment. Then she stood up slowly, still holding on to the wood.

"I'm here," she called. "Stop screaming!"

At once, Chris stopped.

The silence was as terrifying as the darkness.

"Talk! Say something! So I can find you," said Marnie.

"Marnie! Marnie! Marnie!"

"I said talk! Not scream! Talk quietly. Keep talking. I'm coming. ... Ouch! ... It's okay, I just stubbed my toe. Keep talking. ... There, is that you?"

"Marnie, I'm scared," sobbed Chris. "I can't see the way out."

"Don't be scared. We'll find the way. Just grab hold of my parka. ... That's right. ... No, wait! Did you drop your load?"

"Yes."

"Can you find it?"

"In the dark? Down there?" Chris' voice squeaked with fright.

"Yes! I don't want to come back here again! Pick up as much as you can."

"Can you help me?"

"I can't without putting mine down." Fear made Marnie's voice shrill. Chris sobbed. "Oh, okay," she said.

She laid her bundle on her toes so she wouldn't lose it and felt around for Chris' load. Slowly, her eyes were becoming used to the darkness. She

30

could make out the shape of Chris beside her. She picked up a few pieces. A tapping sound began. It sounded like the claws of an animal. Was something going to leap on her back?

She pushed the pile at him. "That's enough. Let's go."

"Where's the stairs?" asked Chris.

"This way. Stick close."

With elbows touching, they shuffled along the cement floor.

Bump!

"Here's the stairs," said Marnie. "Now find the bottom one."

"I might fall off," said Chris.

"No, you won't!" answered Marnie sharply. "There! I've got my elbow on the railing. Now, you stay right beside me and we'll go up together. Ready? Don't drop anything."

Feeling with their feet for each step, they climbed in the pitch darkness. Marnie could feel her heart pounding. When it seemed they must be very near the top, her heart almost stopped. A faint light was flickering ahead.

"Marrrr ..." Chris began to scream.

"It's our fire," she said quickly.

"Oh," breathed Chris.

They stumbled up the rest of the steps, raced across the room and tumbled into their shelter.

＊　＊　＊

THE CITY IN THE STORM

The wind that knocked down the power pole and left Marnie and Chris in the dark was doing other frightening things.

Out on Pembina Highway, it built up a drift, centimetre by centimetre, over a stalled car holding four people. At one time, it swept the corner of Portage and Main Streets all clean of snow, only to blow it back in impassable drifts an hour later. At the airport, it flipped over and smashed many small planes. It blew down power lines and chimneys. It changed the landscape by building hills of snow where no hills had ever been. It took the breath from people's mouths, so that they had to go indoors. Little by little, the city came to a stop.

City Council set up the Emergency Measures Organization to direct volunteer snowmobile drivers who could transport essential workers, deliver medicine, and take food to old people and babies.

One radio station stayed on the air all night. It broadcast orders, advice and messages. It kept reminding people about the Carder children.

❋ ❋ ❋ ❋ ❋ ❋ ❋

Chapter Seven

Grandpa's Story

The children sat close together and watched the fire in silence for a while. If they looked behind them, they saw frightening, leaping shadows in the dark room. It was better not to look.

After a few minutes, Chris complained that his feet were itchy. He pulled off his right boot. He dragged off his wet sock and scratched and scratched and scratched.

"Ouch, ouch, ouch!" he said.

"Stop that!" Marnie said. "You'll make it bleed soon. Here."

She took down one of the dry scarfs and rubbed his foot.

"Ah!" sighed Chris. "Dry the other one."

His sister wrapped each of his feet in one of the warm scarfs. She hung his socks from the mantelpiece and propped his boots near the fire.

"Keep the scarfs on 'til your socks are dry," she said.

"Okay, bossy-boss."

Marnie made a face at him.

"Let's play families," she said.

Families was a guessing game Marnie had made up long ago. One person would think of a family and list all the children in order of age. Then the other person had to guess the family. It was a good game to play in bed

Chris said, "Boy, girl, boy."

That was easy. He always began with their next door neighbours in Victoria.

"Johnsons," said Marnie. "My turn. Boy, boy, boy."

"Grandpa and his brothers!"

"Right!"

They played the game until they ran out of families they both knew. Next Marnie said they would tell stories.

"Not ghost stories!" said Chris.

"No, nice stories. Happy ones."

She told *Cinderella* and he told *The Little Engine That Could.*

At last they were tired of stories and guessing games.

"I wish there was a T.V. It must be time for cartoons," Chris said.

Marnie sighed. Every afternoon, she and Chris would lie on the floor in front of the T.V., while Mummy made supper in the kitchen. Chris nearly always had a toy car or truck in his hand and he raced it back and forth in front of the set until she got mad. Too bad he didn't have any of his toys here.

"Chris, why don't we pretend some of these pieces of wood are cars?"

"Okay!"

He picked up pieces of different sizes. Handing two small ones to Marnie, he said, "Here's two cars. And here's a truck and a bus and another car for me. Where can we make a road?"

34

Marnie picked up one of the sticks that had fallen out of the fire. With the black end she drew a line on the plywood floor.

"Neat!" yelled Chris.

He took the stick from her and drew a network of roads. He built overpasses with laths and made a garage out of a heavy piece of cardboard. As he crawled back and forth from one side of the shelter to the other, the scarfs pulled off his feet and trailed behind him. Marnie made him put on his socks and boots again.

"Why!" he asked. "Are we going home?" He looked up at the back window. "Oh, look how dark it is! We better go!"

"Don't be dumb," said Marnie. "Hear the wind? We can't go home in a blizzard."

"Is this a blizzard?" asked Chris in great surprise.

"Of course it is, you nut!"

"Grandpa was once in a blizzard," he said. "He told me."

"Yes, I know. He told me, too."

"He nearly died," said Chris. "Are we going to die?"

"No! We're not! Grandpa was outside in the storm. We're inside. And he didn't have a fire and we do. Don't you remember his story?"

" Yes, I do," answered Chris. "He was going home from school on the prairie and it was snowing and then a blizzard came and the snow got deeper and deeper and deeper."

"And the pony stumbled into a hole and Grandpa fell off," said Marnie.

"Let me tell! Grandpa walked and walked and walked and then he sat down to rest and the snow covered him all over and he didn't want to get up but he did and he was so tired he couldn't move. And his dad came back with the pony and took him home."

Marnie finished the story. "And Grandpa was so stiff they laid him across two chairs and used him for a piano bench."

"Is that true?" asked Chris.

"Not the last part," Marnie answered, with a smile. Then she stopped smiling. "But it is true that people can freeze to death. We mustn't go to sleep. And we mustn't let the fire go out. If we're careful, we can keep it going 'til morning."

"Til morning!" said Chris. "Will the blizzard last all night?"

"I don't know. But we couldn't go home in the dark anyway."

"All night!" Chris said again. "I might starve to death!"

"No, you won't. It takes a long time to die of starvation. Mummy will find us long before that," Marnie said firmly.

❄   ❄   ❄

MRS. BLEWETT

The Carders lived in the middle of a row of new townhouses at the edge of the city. Mrs. Carder hadn't met many of the neighbours and she didn't know the grey-haired women who knocked on her door at five o'clock.

"I live two doors down," she puffed. "I'm Sadie Blewett, and that's the right name for a day like this! No word of the kiddies, is there? Well, I've come to stay with you as long as you need me."

Mrs. Carder whispered, "Oh, Mrs. Blewett! I'm so frightened!"

"Of course you are! So am I. A blizzard is something to be scared of, I can tell you! But, don't give up hope, dear. There's dozens of places those kids could have got to. They can't come home in this." She waved her big arm toward the window. "You wouldn't want them to."

"No, but I'm afraid they're out in it."

"Well, we won't think about that. Let's make some hot soup and sit by the radio and talk. I'll just get my knitting."

❄ ❄ ❄ ❄ ❄ ❄ ❄

Chapter Eight

Marnie's Dream

The next few hours were very hard for Marnie. When Chris was tired of car games she had to think of other things to do. Because it was so cold and dark in the rest of the room, they couldn't move away from the fire. They did sitting up and stretching exercises until Chris said that so much work made him hungrier than ever. He also needed to go to the toilet badly. So did Marnie. There was no toilet bowl in the bathroom, only a drain hole in the floor. They used that and Marnie tried not to think about what Mummy would say.

Back in their nook, Marnie told stories again. They talked about their old home in Victoria and friends there. That made them both sad.

She added more wood on the fire and then put her arms around Chris. He fell asleep against her side. She wondered what her mother was doing. She would be lonely, too, as well as worried. Maybe they shouldn't have stopped at this house. Maybe they should have tried to reach home. She imagined what it would have been like, if they had gone home. Mummy would be standing at the front window, looking out, waiting and worrying. Marnie would stagger out of the storm, dragging her little brother, who couldn't walk any farther. And Mummy would see her coming and run out without her coat and she'd pick Chris up. Inside it would be warm. Mummy would be proud of her.

Marnie shook the daydreams away. Chris? Was he cold? She felt his cheeks. They were warm enough. She poked him gently and he grunted at her. He was alive. She eased him down to the floor, pulled up his parka hood and slipped on his dry mittens. Let him sleep.

How was she to keep herself awake? She stood up and walked the few paces between the upright doors. Sometimes the wind sounded like a wild animal snarling. A shadow cast by the firelight looked like a wolf about to pounce. She quickly sat down again, close to her sleeping brother.

She recited a poem Miss Maxwell had made them learn yesterday. It seemed weeks ago! Then she said her times table. She tried to make up a limerick. She was so sleepy, she couldn't remember the first line by the time she got to the fifth.

Slipping down beside Chris, she cuddled close to him. I'll rest here for a minute, she thought. I won't go to sleep because if I do we'll freeze. So, I won't go to sleep.

40

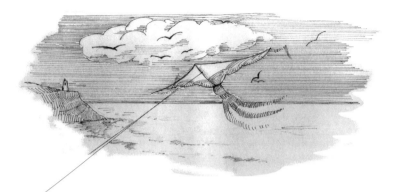

A minute later, she was fast asleep.

She began to dream. In her dream, she was back in Victoria. It was summertime. She and Chris were on the beach just three blocks from their home. They had often taken their lunch and spent most of the day there during the school holidays while their mother worked. Mrs. Carder paid for a high school girl to look after them, but she spent most of her time looking at boys. That's what Grandpa said, when he came to visit. So, Marnie took care of Chris herself.

The high school girl was not in the dream. At first Mummy was there as well as Grandpa and Grandma. Then they all disappeared and Jenny, Marnie's best friend, was there instead. The three of them, dressed in bathing suits, were playing at the edge of the sea. They let the waves almost touch their toes before jumping back. Seagulls were screaming overhead.

Suddenly, several gulls swooped down toward the waves, dipped their bills into the water and soared up

41

again to the sky. There, they turned into kites, and drifted toward the point. Laughing, Jenny and Marnie raced along the hard sand trying to keep up to them. Then the kites became gulls again and flew out to sea. Marnie looked back and saw they had come a long, long way. She couldn't see Chris. Was he lost? What would Mummy say? She tried to run back but the sand slowed her down so that she seemed to be barely moving.

The sun beat down. In the far distance, she spotted Chris. He had no hat on. He'd get sunstroke and be sick. She had to take him out of the sun. He was too hot. She must hurry. Chris was too hot. No, that wasn't right. He was cold. She was all mixed up. She had to save Chris. He was too hot. No, Chris was cold.

Marnie woke up shivering.

She knew she had been dreaming, but she didn't, at first, know why she was so cold. When she remembered where she was, she was surprised at how dark it was. She couldn't even see Chris, although she could feel him beside her.

❈ ❈ ❈

Chapter Nine

TRAPPED

Why was it so dark? It was hard to think. When she had closed her eyes to rest for a minute, the fire-light had been flickering on the ceiling.

Of course! The fire! Marnie struggled to sit up. The fire was out! They would freeze to death without a fire. Fearfully, she patted at her brother until she found his face. His cheek was ice cold. She shook him. He didn't make a sound. Was he dead? She wanted to scream at him to wake up. At the same time, she was afraid to find out that he couldn't wake.

How long had the fire been out? Marnie climbed over Chris and held her hand out toward the fireplace. There was no warmth, only an icy current of air through the open draft. The wind was still whistling at the top of the chimney.

A big lump rose in Marnie's throat.

"Mummy," she said, in a whimper.

But Mummy wasn't here. There was only herself and Chris in the pitch dark. She must light the fire again, but that meant reaching out in the darkness for the fuel. Still, she had to have some light and she must warm Chris. She forced herself to feel around until she found scraps of paper and pieces of wood.

Her movements made puffs of ash fly up from the dead fire. She sneezed. It was horrible feeling around in the dark! If she lit just one match she would be able to see. They had put the matchbook back on the mantelpiece. At first, she couldn't make her hand reach out. Who knew what she might touch? But it was even more frightening not to be able to see. She found the mantle and felt along it. At last, her cold hand touched the book. Her fingers were so numb, they knocked it to the floor.

She shivered. She wished Chris would wake and keep her company. But first, she'd better light the fire or he'd only complain about the cold. She heard the matchbook hit the floor and she soon had it in her hand.

There were five matches. She ripped one out and with trembling fingers stroked it on the package. Nothing happened. She had rubbed off the head instead of lighting it.

Don't waste any more, she told herself firmly.

The second match lit and gave her a few seconds of welcome light before going out. Quickly she piled up the paper, the wood and some small, unburned pieces from the first fire.

She struck another match and set the paper alight. It burned quickly and brightly for a minute and then died.

The darkness seemed blacker than ever. During the short time of light, Marnie had seen the cardboard that Chris had used for a garage. How long ago that seemed! She used it as a base to rebuild her pile. With the second last match, she tried again. A piece of

44

paper caught fire. Crouched on the hearth, she fed the flame with more paper and bits of partly-burned wood until the cardboard caught. Then it lighted the bigger wood.

When the fire was burning well, she made herself turn to Chris. He was lying curled into a ball with his face toward the fire. She touched his cheek again. It was still cold. When she took her hand away, she was startled to see black streaks on his face. What did that mean? Then she looked at her hands and saw they were dirty from the fire.

Angry with herself for being frightened, she shook Chris roughly. He grunted. She shook harder. He uncurled and kicked out with one leg. She called his name. She rolled him over. He pushed at her with his hands, still with his eyes closed.

"Wake up, Chris! Wake up!"

"Go 'way," he mumbled. "Lemmme sleep!"

"No! You mustn't sleep! Wake up!"

She shook him harder. He flopped over, kicking and hitting at her. He opened one eye just a slit.

"Lemmelone," he said. "I wanna sleep."

"Chris," Marnie begged, "wake up and walk around a bit. You'll freeze there."

But he wouldn't wake and she wasn't strong enough to drag him up.

She stood with her hands on her hips looking down at him. He was alive. And he had moved enough to warm himself a little. The fire was burning well and she wouldn't let it go out again.

45

Another two hours passed. Marnie dozed but stayed awake enough to keep the fire going. The worst part was the loneliness. Sometimes she poked Chris, just to make him grunt at her.

Time seemed endless.

Once, when she woke from a doze, she put the last piece of insulation on the fire and watched it catch fire. It smoked for a moment and the smoke made her cough. She rubbed her eyes. She could see the walls of the room! She looked toward the back window.

It's morning! she thought. She listened. No wind.

"The storm's over," she shouted. "Chris! Chris! Wake up!"

"Huh?" said Chris.

"The storm's over! Listen. No wind."

Chris scrambled up. Because he was stiff, he staggered against the low wall of their shelter. It fell down. He beat his sister in a race to the front door. His mittened hand slipped on the doorknob.

"Let me!" said Marnie.

She grabbed the cold metal and twisted.

Nothing happened.

"I'll do it!" Chris yelled.

They twisted and pulled and pulled and twisted. The door would not open.

"It's stuck," said Chris with tears in his voice.

Marnie slumped against the wall.

"Probably frozen," she said sadly. "We can't get out."

"The back door!" yelled Chris.

He ran through the kitchen. Marnie stayed where she was. She remembered seeing the back door the day before. It was nailed shut. All the windows, except for the front picture window which didn't open, were much too high for them to reach. The front window was completely covered by a snowdrift.

Chris was crying when he came back. "What are we going to do, Marnie?" he asked.

* * *

MRS. SAWCHUK

On the morning after the storm, Mrs. Annie Sawchuk put the coffee pot on the stove. She was alone in the house. Her daughter and husband had both phoned the evening before to say they were snowed in at their places of work. Turning to look out the window, she smiled at the blue sky. Then her eyes opened wide.

A wisp of white smoke drifted from the chimney next door.

She gasped and ran to the phone. Her fingers trembled as she dialed.

"Emergency Organization?" she said. "My name is Mrs. Sawchuk and I live on Marigold Avenue. I can't get out on account of the snow. No, no, no! I'm okay! Listen while I tell you! No one lives next door to me, but there's smoke coming from the chimney. Could it be those little lost children I heard about on the radio?"

Mr. Dave Arnold lived just three blocks down Marigold Avenue. He owned a snowmobile and was registered with the Emergency Measures Organization. Ten minutes after Mrs. Sawchuk's phone call, Mr. Arnold sped off to investigate.

❧ ❧ ❧ ❧ ❧ ❧

Chapter Ten

RESCUE

Marnie looked at her brother. She didn't know what they were going to do. Maybe she could hold Chris up and push him out of the kitchen window. The trouble was, she'd still be inside. He was only seven years old and the snow was deep. Could he go for help by himself? Would it be better to stay together?

She put her hand on his shoulder.

"Chris," she said, "do you think ..." Then she stopped. She tilted her head toward the door.

"Listen! Listen!" she said.

"What?" asked Chris. "I don't hear ... Oh! Oh! A motor!"

"Help!" yelled Marnie. "Help! Help!"

Chris beat on the door with his hands and feet.

"We're here! We can't get out!" he shouted.

The noise of the engine came very close and stopped.

"I wish we could see," said Marnie. "Help! Help!" She, too, pounded on the door. "Keep yelling, Chris."

"Help! We can't get out! Help!"

"I hear you," said a deep voice.

Tears filled Marnie's eyes. She tried to hug Chris but he wouldn't stand still. He ran to the big window and back to the door.

"Is it Mummy?" he asked.

"It's someone," Marnie answered with a laugh.

For a few minutes they heard nothing. Where was the man? Then there was the sound of metal hitting wood.

"He's digging," said Chris.

They waited in silence, staring at the blank door.

"Hello?" shouted the voice.

"Hello," they answered eagerly.

"Stand back from the door!"

Marnie grabbed Chris and pulled him away.

Bang! The door burst open.

Halfway up the opening, a big man crouched in a snowdrift. Except for his eyes, he was completely covered in blue nylon.

"Hi," he said. "Are you the Carder kids?"

"Yes," said Marnie, wondering how he knew.

The man jumped into the hall, bringing a lot of snow with him. He looked swiftly around the room and then back at the children. He pushed back his hood, took off his ski mask and smiled.

"I'm Mr. Arnold," he said. "Are you okay?"

"We're cold," said Chris. "And hungry. Did you come to rescue us?"

"I sure did. Wrap yourselves up and we'll get you home to your mother."

"Oh, boy!" said Chris.

It took only a few minutes on the snowmobile to reach the Carder home but Chris talked so fast and so loud that Mr. Arnold heard all about building the fire and making the fort and the lights going out.

50

"Smart kids!" he said, when he turned off the engine.

Just as Marnie had imagined, her mother was standing at the window and saw them pull up. Before they were out of the machine, she had the door open. They stumbled into her arms.

After a little while, Marnie could hear Mr. Arnold and a lady talking. Then the lady went out and closed the door. Mummy didn't even hear because she was so busy undoing their snowsuits and hugging and crying over them.

At last, she sat down in the big chair and pulled Chris on to her lap. One arm went around Marnie who was perched on the wide arm of the chair.

51

"I'll be going," said Mr. Arnold.

"Oh dear, I never even thanked you! Or Mrs. Blewett either!"

"No need for thanks," he said. "I'm just glad to see the kids back with you. Don't get up. I'll let myself out."

He stopped with his hand on the doorknob. He gave Mrs. Carder the kind of look grownups exchange when they want to keep something from the kids.

"The house they were in," he said, "that's the last house before the open prairie."

Mummy shivered. She hugged both children closer.

"They're safe now," she whispered into Chris' hair.

❊ ❊ ❊

Much later, Chris called sleepily up to his sister from the bottom bunk.

"Marnie?"

"Mmmmmmm?"

"It was more fun riding in the snowmobile than seeing Bobby's cars. I bet he doesn't have a hundred anyway."

Marnie giggled. "You're a nut. A big, fat, Brazil nut! Go to sleep, nut!"

The End

About the Author

Constance Horne was born in Winnipeg. She taught high school at Minnedosa, Manitoba, Nelson BC, and Vancouver.

Her other children's titles include: *The Accidental Orphan* (1998), *Emily Carr's Woo* (1995), *Trapped by Coal* (1994), *The Jo Boy Deserts and Other Stories* (1992) and *Nykola and Granny* (1989).

She is married with four grown children and two grandsons. She presently lives in Victoria.

About the Illustrator

Lori McGregor McCrae is a freelance artist living in Edmonton with her husband John and two children, Teague and Georgia.

She holds a BFA degree from the University of Alberta and works as a commissioned portrait artist.

If you liked this book...
you might enjoy these other Hodgepog books:

Read them yourself in grades 4-5, or read them to younger kids.

Ben and the Carrot Predicament
by Mar'ce Merrell, illustrated by Barbara Hartmann
ISBN 1-895836-54-9   Price $4.95

Getting Rid of Mr. Ribitus
by Alison Lohans, illustrated by Barbara Hartmann
ISBN 1-895836-53-0   Price $5.95

A Real Farm Girl
by Susan Ioannou, illustrated by James Rozak
ISBN 1-895836-52-2   Price $6.95

A Gift for Johnny Know-It-All
by Mary Woodbury, illustrated by Barbara Hartmann
ISBN 1-895836-27-1   Price $5.95

Mill Creek Kids
by Colleen Heffernan, illustrated by Sonja Zacharias
ISBN 1-895836-40-9   Price $5.95

Arly and Spike
by Luanne Armstrong, illustrated by Chao Yu
ISBN 1-895836-37-9   Price $4.95

A Friend for Mr. Granville
by Gillian Richardson, illustrated by Claudette MacLean
ISBN 1-895836-38-7   Price $5.95

Maggie and Shine
by Luanne Armstrong, illustrated by Dorothy Woodend
ISBN 1-895836-67-0   Price $6.95

Butterfly Gardens
by Judith Benson, Illustrated by Lori McGregor McCrae
ISBN 1-895836-71-9   Price $5.95

and for readers in grades 1-2, or to read to pre-schoolers

Sebastian's Promise
by Gwen Molnar, Illustrated by Kendra McCleskey
ISBN 1-895836-65-4   Price $4.95

Summer With Sebastian
by Gwen Molnar, illustrated by Kendra McCleskey
ISBN 1-895836-39-5   Price $4.95

The Noise in Grandma's Attic
by Judith Benson, illustrated by Shane Hill
ISBN 1-895836-55-7   Price $4.95

SUNSHINE HILLS ELEMENTARY SCHOOL
11285 BOND BLVD.
DELTA, B.C.   V4E 1N3